The Barber's Clever Wife

White Wolves Series Consultant: Sue Ellis,
Centre for Literacy in Primary Education

This book can be used in the White Wolves Guided Reading
programme for independent readers in Year 5

First published 2004 by
A & C Black
Bloomsbury Publishing Plc
50 Bedford Square
London
WC1B 3DP

www.acblack.com

ISBN 978-0-7136-6860-5

A CIP catalogue for this book is available from the British Library.

This book is produced using paper that is made from wood grown
in managed, sustainable forests. It is natural, renewable and
recyclable. The logging and manufacturing processes conform
to the environmental regulations of the country of origin.

Printed and bound by CPI Group (UK) Ltd, Croydon, CR0 4YY

5 7 9 10 8 6

The Barber's Clever Wife

Retold by Narinder Dhami

Illustrated by Katja Bandlow

A & C Black • London

Contents

Chapter One

Many years ago, in the middle of the flat, green plains of the Punjab, stood a large, sprawling village of square, flat-roofed houses. The village was surrounded by sugar cane fields, and in the distance could be glimpsed the tall, snow-capped peaks of the Himalayan mountains.

In a tumbledown house on the edge of this village lived a man called Bulbul and his wife, Ruby.

Bulbul was a barber by trade. However, everyone agreed that he was undoubtedly the worst barber in the whole world.

Bulbul was unable to shave his customers' beards or cut their hair without nicking their faces or snipping the tops of their ears. His customers would run out of the barber's shop, shouting in pain, blood streaming down their faces, their hair or beard only half-trimmed.

Everyone in the village knew what Bulbul was like. The old men would gather in the square to chew betel nuts and complain loudly about the barber.

"I'll let my beard grow down to my knees before I'll allow that fool to trim it again!" they would mutter.

Eventually, Bulbul's customers began to stay away. Without customers, he had no way of earning money and soon he and Ruby began to sink into poverty.

To tell the truth, Bulbul was extremely lazy, and, given the choice, he preferred not to work at all.

He enjoyed sitting at home in the courtyard, shaded by the spreading mango tree, watching the monkeys swinging through the branches by their tails. But his wife Ruby was having none of it.

"We simply can't go on like this," she

said firmly one evening. They were out in the courtyard as the sun, a great flaming ball of red, sank down in the sky. Ruby was vigorously pounding wheat between millstones to make flour. Bulbul was dozing, stretched out on a bedroll.

Ruby glared at her husband. "When this wheat's gone, we've none left, and no money to buy more," she pointed out. "What are we going to eat then?"

Bulbul yawned widely, and scratched his tatty white turban. "Oh, something's bound to turn up," he muttered.

"Is that so?" Ruby snapped. "Well, I'm not planning to starve to death! You'll just have to go out and beg."

“Beg?” Bulbul repeated warily. He considered that for a moment. Begging sounded much easier than cutting hair every day.

Also, he was a little scared of Ruby. She had a tongue as sharp as a knife, so it was much wiser to do what she said, without argument. "How do I do that?"

"I have it all worked out," Ruby said triumphantly, dusting off her floury hands. "The King's daughter is getting married tomorrow, so there'll be a great wedding feast at the palace. On such a happy day, the King will be glad to give alms to beggars."

"If you say so," Bulbul agreed. He yawned again. "I'll go tomorrow sometime."

"You'll go early in the morning as soon as the sun rises," Ruby ordered sternly, giving her lazy husband a poke in the ribs.

So next day when the dawn broke,

streaking the pale blue sky with pink and gold, Ruby turned Bulbul out of bed, and sent him on his way.

It was quite a distance to the palace. Bulbul wandered along the dusty roads, keeping under the mango trees out of the hot sun. Every so often he hitched a lift from a passing hay cart. At last, hot and tired, he reached the city walls.

The city was busy and bustling. All around Bulbul, people jostled and pushed each other, the shopkeepers shouted out their wares and people drove their cattle to sell them at the market.

In the middle of the city Bulbul could see the King's palace. The white marble domes, towers and minarets, inlaid with rich gems, gleamed and dazzled in the blazing sun.

Bulbul wandered through the golden gates into the palace gardens. The wedding feast had begun, and people were thronging to join the celebrations. The gates were open to all, even the poorest beggar. The King's courtiers, dressed in their finest silks and satins, arrived riding their white horses or seated on their richly-decorated elephants.

A band of musicians sat beside a marble fountain, and filled the air with music. There were dancers and acrobats to entertain the crowds. Flowers bloomed wherever the eye could see, and the air was rich with the sweet scent of jasmine.

Bulbul was dazzled by all this beauty and colour but he was tired out from the journey. He yawned till his jaw cracked. He longed to stretch out on the lawns, where peacocks strutted, spreading their blue and green tail feathers to the sun, and watch everything that was going on around him.

But he remembered what Ruby had said. With a sigh, he joined the long, long queue of people who were waiting for an audience with the King.

The King was seated beneath a gold-fringed canopy, surrounded by his courtiers.

Two servants stood either side of the jewelled throne, fanning the King with enormous palm leaves to keep him cool in the midday sun.

The King was in an excellent mood. His youngest child and favourite daughter was today marrying a prince from the next province, whose family were extremely wealthy.

So when a tubby little man in a tatty white turban stepped forward and asked for help, the King smiled and nodded graciously.

"What kind of help are you looking for, my man?" he asked.

"Sire, I can't earn any money," explained Bulbul. "So my wife has sent me here to beg." He sighed. "Please, give me something to keep her quiet."

The courtiers laughed.

"Of course," the King agreed. "What would you like?"

Bulbul looked puzzled. Ruby hadn't told him what to ask for, and he had no idea what to say.

By this time the courtiers were in fits of laughter.

"He's come all this way to beg, and he doesn't know what to beg for!" one chuckled.

The King held up his hand to silence them. "What about a piece of land?" he asked. "That's something you can pass on to your sons."

Bulbul nodded gratefully. "Thank you, your Majesty."

The King turned to one of his guards. "Give this man a piece of waste land outside the city walls," he ordered. He turned to Bulbul. "And good luck to you."

Bulbul began the long journey

home, feeling very pleased with himself. He was sure Ruby would be thrilled with the King's gift.

"Begging is a much easier way of earning a living than trimming people's beards!" he thought with satisfaction. "And the King has many sons and daughters. Every time there's a wedding, I can go and beg. I'll never have to work again!"

Back in the village, Ruby was waiting impatiently for her husband, although she didn't hold out much hope that he would bring anything with him. It was much more likely that he had stopped to rest along the way, and fallen asleep in the sun!

But at last, as the moon appeared in the evening sky, she heard the slap-slap of his sandals on the dusty road. Ruby flung down the sari she was mending, and dashed to meet him.

"What happened?" she cried. "Did you see the King? Did he give you anything?"

"Oh, yes," Bulbul replied. "I told you something would turn up."

"What is it?" Ruby wanted to know. "Something we can sell? A jewel? Or did he give you a gold coin?"

Bulbul drew himself up to full height. "He gave me a piece of waste land outside the city walls," he said proudly.

Ruby's face fell.

"What!" she shrieked. "A piece of land? What good is land to us? We don't have a bullock, or a plough or any other tools!" And with a moan of dismay, she buried her head in her hands.

Bulbul rolled his eyes. He'd done what Ruby had asked him to, and this was the result. Women! Ruby was never happy.

"Let me think." Ruby glanced up at her husband, a determined look on her face. "There must be a way for us to make money from this piece of land."

"How?" asked Bulbul helplessly.

"Leave it to me," Ruby replied, her eyes gleaming. "I shall think of a plan!"

Chapter Two

"So this is our land."

Ruby stood outside the city walls and gazed around her. It was the following morning. She had hurried Bulbul out of bed very early, ignoring his complaints, and they had set off for the city.

Ruby paced up and down the piece of land. Despite scolding Bulbul earlier, she was quite impressed.

"It's much bigger than I expected,"

she said. She knelt, picked up a clod of earth and crumbled it between her fingers. "The soil's good, too. Dark and fertile."

"But we don't have any tools, so we can't till or sow or harvest a crop," Bulbul reminded her. He yawned, scratching his turban. "Can we go home now?"

Ruby shook her head. "Watch me closely," she said, smiling widely, "and do exactly as I do."

Ruby began to walk up and down the land, a frown on her face. Then she stopped and stared hard at a certain piece of earth. She looked worried and excited at the same time. She put her hands on her hips, and tapped her foot as if she was thinking hard, and trying to make a decision.

Bulbul had no idea what Ruby was up to. He stared hard at the same piece of land, but couldn't see anything out of the ordinary. He didn't have a clue what Ruby was looking at.

Footsteps sounded behind them. An elderly man was coming along the dirt track, pushing a handcart. Immediately, Ruby sat down on a clump of grass and began humming a tune, looking innocent. The man passed by. Then Ruby sprang to her feet and began staring anxiously at the land again.

Bulbul was utterly bewildered. The

same thing happened again a few minutes later when a small child ran past, bowling a hoop. Again Ruby sat down again and hummed. Then, when the child had gone, she began pacing the land again.

"What are we staring at?" asked Bulbul, very puzzled. "And why did we stop when the old man and the child went by?"

Ruby shrugged. "Forget about the old man and the boy," she told him. "We're not waiting for them."

"We're waiting for someone?" Bulbul repeated. "Who?"

"I don't know," Ruby replied. "I'll know when I see them! Just do as I do."

By now Bulbul was completely confused, but he was too lazy to enquire further. Frowning hard, he followed his wife up and down their land, staring at the earth.

When someone went by, they both sat down and hummed. Then, when they were alone again, Ruby hauled Bulbul back on his feet to continue pacing up and down.

Ruby and Bulbul's behaviour was already beginning to attract attention. Near the city walls was a huge wood, thick with tall trees. It was home to a notorious band of seven thieves, who were hated by all the honest people of the city. The thieves made their living by robbing travellers, and stealing anything they could lay their hands on.

Their leader, Karan, had noticed Ruby and Bulbul in the distance, and had begun watching them. Puzzled by their behaviour, he called the rest of his robber band to the edge of the wood to take a look.

As Ruby walked up and down, dragging Bulbul with her, she noticed the thieves peering out from behind the trees. Ruby smiled to herself.

"There's something funny going on there," Karan said to the others, twirling his huge black moustache. "And there might be rich pickings in it for us, boys. Let's keep watch and find out what they're doing!"

The six thieves grinned, showing rotted and blackened teeth.

The seven thieves watched Ruby and Bulbul all day from the shelter of the trees. The husband and wife's behaviour never varied. They paced, they stared, they frowned, and when anyone went by they sat and hummed a tune. The thieves couldn't understand it.

"This is sending me mad!" Karan roared furiously, as the sun began to set. "What is that pair up to?" He turned to one of his band, a short squat man with a ragged beard. "Mohan, go and find out what they're doing. But be careful. Don't let them suspect anything."

Mohan slipped out from between the trees and made his way towards Ruby and Bulbul. Ruby spotted him straightaway, and nudged Bulbul in the ribs. Immediately the pair sat down and began to hum.

"Hello, friends!" Mohan said with a

broad smile. “I couldn’t help noticing that a moment ago you were searching for something. May I give you a hand to look for whatever you’ve lost?”

“Oh!” Ruby looked flustered. “No, but thank you all the same.”

“It must be very hot and thirsty work,” Mohan said, sitting down beside them. “Here, have a drink.”

He handed Bulbul the water bottle clipped to his belt. “You know, the sun is going to set soon.” Mohan glanced up at the pink sky as Bulbul drank greedily. “Why don’t you let me help you?”

Ruby hesitated. “That’s very kind, but really there’s no need.”

“Three pairs of eyes are better than

two," Mohan pointed out.

Ruby thought for a moment. "Well, if you really want to help," she said, "we'd be very grateful." She lowered her voice. "But you mustn't breathe a word to anyone of what I'm going to tell you. We have to be careful – there are so many thieves about!"

"Oh I understand," Mohan agreed, trying to look as honest as he could.

"Many years ago my grandfather buried five pots of gold on this land," Ruby explained. "My husband and I are trying to decide where to start digging for them."

"We are?" Bulbul asked in amazement.

"Oh, I see!" Mohan just about stopped himself rubbing his hands with glee. "Then of course I'll help you. But it's already getting dark. Why don't you go home and come back tomorrow?"

Ruby yawned. "Yes, I think you're right," she agreed. "After all, the gold will still be there."

"That's what *you* think!" Mohan muttered to himself.

"Ruby," said Bulbul in a puzzled voice, as they set off on the long walk back to the village, "why didn't you mention your grandfather's gold before?"

Ruby smiled. "There isn't a single gold coin hidden in that land, as far as I know," she replied.

Bulbul looked even more confused. "So why did you say there was?"

"Wait and see!" Ruby told him, hardly able to stop herself laughing.

As soon as Ruby and Bulbul were out of sight, Mohan tore across the fields to the wood. Karan and the other thieves were waiting impatiently.

"Gold!" Mohan gasped, out of breath. "There's gold buried in that land. Five pots full!"

Karan's eyes lit up. "Gold!" he yelled. "Get the shovels and pickaxes, boys. That gold's ours!"

The men rushed to get their tools, then they headed over to Ruby and

Bulbul's land. It was dark now, but they took oil lamps to light their way. They all set to with a will, digging and turning and tilling the soil. It was extremely hard work, but they didn't give up.

"Keep going, boys!" Karan urged them. "Think of all that lovely gold waiting for us!"

Sweating and cursing, the thieves worked on, carefully sifting every bit of soil. By morning they had dug the whole field, and broken up every clod of earth. But they hadn't found a single gold coin.

"You idiot!" Karan growled, cuffing Mohan round the head. "You must have been mistaken."

Groaning and rubbing their aching backs, the thieves plodded wearily back to the wood. They all fell asleep immediately, tired out from the hard work. So they didn't see Ruby and Bulbul arrive at the city walls a few hours later, pushing a handcart piled with sacks.

Bulbul's eyes almost popped out of his head when he saw the tilled field.

"It's a miracle!" he cried, falling to his knees in wonder.

Ruby put her hands on her hips and roared with laughter. Her plan had worked beautifully.

"But what are we going to do now?" asked Bulbul. "We don't have any money to buy seeds."

Ruby patted the sacks on the cart. "Yes, we do," she replied gleefully. "I went out and borrowed some rice seed from a farmer in our village last night, while you were snoring your head off!"

Bulbul looked aghast. "But we can't pay him!"

"Not yet," replied Ruby. "But when we've sowed and harvested the rice crop, I've promised to repay him with interest."

This was exactly what happened. The rice crop grew and flourished in the well-tilled field. A few months later, Ruby and Bulbul had a huge crop to harvest. Even after repaying the farmer, they had a whole pot of gold coins for themselves. The couple had never been so wealthy. Ruby was thrilled her plan had worked so well, but she couldn't help wondering what the thieves would do, when they found out that they'd been tricked.

All this time the thieves had been watching what was happening from their hideout in the woods. They were not quite as stupid as Bulbul, but nevertheless, it took them quite a while to realise that they had been duped. When they did realise, however, they were sizzling with fury.

"We dug and tilled that field," Karan raged. "So those gold coins should be ours!"

He rounded up his men, and they marched off to Ruby and Bulbul's village.

Ruby was sweeping the courtyard when the thieves arrived. Bulbul was asleep in the shade as usual, but he woke up when the thieves appeared. He looked very nervous when he saw the band of cut-throats. Ruby was a little nervous too, but she didn't show it. She'd expected the thieves to turn up sooner or later.

"Yes?" she asked coolly. "May I help you?"

"Well, it's like this." Karan drew himself up and twirled his moustache. "I and my band of – er – friends here were the ones who tilled your land. Now you've become rich because of our labours." He took a step towards Ruby, his tone menacing. "So hand over your big pot of gold coins, if you know what's good for you!"

Ruby laughed. "I told you there was gold in the ground, didn't I?" she said to Mohan. "Well, I was right!" She lifted her broom and waved it at the thieves. "Now off you go because you're not getting a penny!"

The thieves backed their way out of the courtyard, muttering and shaking their fists.

"Fancy being outwitted by a woman!" Karan raged. "If the other bands of thieves in the area hear about this, we'll never live it down!"

"We should take the gold by force," one of them said.

Karan shook his head. "And have the rest of the village come running when they hear her screams? No, I've got a much better idea." He glared at Mohan. "It was your fault that we ended up working so hard for nothing," Karan growled. "So you can be the one to steal that gold this very night!"

Chapter Three

"Who were those men?" asked Bulbul, as Ruby carried on sweeping the courtyard.

"Oh, that was the band of thieves who live in the wood near the city walls," Ruby replied calmly. "They dug and tilled our field, because they thought they would find gold."

"What?" Bulbul gasped. "You mean – you planned it that way?"

"Of course I did!" Ruby replied

impatiently. "And it worked, didn't it? Now they want our gold – but they're certainly not getting it! I'll stop them any way I can." And, thinking hard, she went into the house, leaving Bulbul shaking with fear.

Bulbul jumped to his feet and ran to the courtyard gate. He peered out, up and down the village street, but there was no sign of the thieves. Bulbul heaved a sigh of relief. They'd gone, and the gold was still safe. Now, what was for dinner? Something smelt good.

Bulbul turned and headed back to the house. He didn't notice Mohan slip from the shadows of a nearby doorway and follow him silently into the courtyard. Mohan hid behind the mango tree until Bulbul had gone inside. Then he tiptoed across the courtyard to the house. He could hear Ruby and Bulbul chatting in the kitchen. Quickly, Mohan climbed through the bedroom window, and hid behind a tall cupboard.

"Ruby, do you think the thieves will come back?" Bulbul asked nervously, as he and his wife prepared for bed later that evening.

"Oh, I don't think so," Ruby replied. But she could see a pair of worn and dusty sandals peeping out from underneath the cupboard in the corner. "And even if they did, they'd never find the gold. I've hidden it in a very safe place."

Behind the cupboard Mohan's ears pricked up.

"Where?" asked Bulbul.

"I put the gold in the big jar by the door," Ruby replied, "and I covered it with sweetmeats. No one will ever guess where it is."

"That's what you think!" Mohan muttered softly. Grinning to himself, he waited until Ruby and Bulbul were asleep. Then he tiptoed out from behind the cupboard.

The big brown jar was by the door, just as Ruby had said. Noiselessly, Mohan lifted it into his arms and stole out of the house. The jar was heavy, but he clung on to it firmly as he made his way out of the village and back to the city. There was only a thin sliver of crescent moon, so it was difficult to see the way. But he kept going.

The other thieves were lounging around in the wood, smoking and rolling dice, when Mohan appeared. He was hot and tired out, but triumphant.

"Gold!" he panted. "I've found the gold!"

Karan grabbed the pot eagerly. "At last we've got what's rightfully ours!" he said with glee.

"And there are sweetmeats on top," Mohan added breathlessly. "Give me some, I'm starving!"

"Me too," chorused the other thieves. They all gathered round as Karan divided up the food, and began cramming it into their mouths.

"Urrrgh!" Mohan spluttered, coughing loudly. "Sweetmeats? I've never tasted anything so disgusting!"

"It's horrible!" Karan gasped, spitting a mouthful on to the ground.

"My mouth's on fire!" roared another.

The thieves made a dash for the river to wash their mouths out with water. They blundered around in the dark, bumping into each other and yelling and spitting. Under the light of the burning torches on the city walls, Karan emptied out the pot. The top was filled with vegetable peelings and chilli seeds, mixed with bits of eggshell and lumps of dirt. There was no gold at the bottom either, just some lumps of firewood.

"You idiot!" Karan roared, grabbing Mohan by the neck. "That woman's fooled you again!”

“It’s not my fault,” Mohan whined sulkily.

“You’ll try again tomorrow night,” Karan ordered furiously. “And this time we will get that gold! I’m not going to let a simple village woman get the better of me!”

In the morning, when Ruby awoke, the first thing she did was check to see if the big brown jar was missing. When she saw it was gone, she laughed heartily as she thought of the greedy thieves cramming their mouths with vile-tasting rubbish. But when she told Bulbul what she’d done, he was so petrified, he shook in his shoes.

"B-b-but what if they come back again to take their revenge?" he wailed.

"Then we must be ready for them!" Ruby replied in a determined voice.

That evening, the thieves set off for Ruby and Bulbul's village again. This time, Mohan climbed in through the window and hid under Ruby's bed, while Karan and the rest of the thieves waited in the street outside.

"Ruby," said Bulbul nervously, when they lay down to sleep, "I'm still very worried about the thieves coming back."

"Don't panic," Ruby said calmly. She smiled to herself as she noticed the edge of a grubby white shirt poking out from under her bed. "I've hidden the gold in a much better place than that old pot."

Under the bed Mohan's ears flapped.

"Where?" asked Bulbul.

"In the big mango tree in the courtyard," Ruby replied. "It's safe there."

"That's what you think," Mohan muttered to himself. Again he waited until Ruby and Bulbul were asleep. Then he slipped out of the bedroom, and joined his fellow thieves in the street.

Karan scowled at him. "Well?" he demanded.

Mohan pointed at the mango tree. "The gold's up there," he said smugly.

"I told you I'd find it this time!"

By the light of the moon, Karan could see a large sack hanging from a branch.

"There it is!" he said, rubbing his hands together. "Mohan, you climb up and bring it down."

Immediately, Mohan shinned up the tree, and reached out a hand towards the bag.

But a sudden, buzzing noise made Mohan flinch. A large hornet flew out of the bag, buzzed angrily towards him and stung him viciously on the thigh. Mohan shrieked with pain, and clapped his hand to the bite.

"What're you doing?" Karan called suspiciously. "Are you stealing the gold for yourself?"

"Yes, he is!" shouted one of the other thieves. "I saw him put his hand in his pocket."

"No," Mohan groaned. "I've been stung! This isn't a bag of gold, it's a hornet's nest – OUCH!" But his words were lost in a roar of pain, as another hornet stung him on the chest.

"He's stealing our gold!" Karan hissed angrily. "Quick, boys. Let's stop him!"

The other thieves climbed up the tree as fast as they could. Karan reached the hornet's nest first, and grabbed the bag. Meanwhile, the other robbers all climbed on to the same branch.

There was a deafening C-R-A-C-K. The branch splintered and plunged to the ground, taking the seven thieves and the hornet's nest with it. Immediately a swarm of angry hornets flew out of the nest, buzzing loudly and stinging whatever was in their path. In this case, Karan and his band of thieves.

"Ouch!" they roared. "Ow!"

Bumped, bruised and covered in stings, the thieves took to their heels and ran like the wind, back to the safety of their wood. Ruby peeped out of the window, and laughed to herself as she saw them flee.

"You think you're so clever, barber's wife!" Karan muttered, "but we'll be back to get our revenge!"

Chapter Four

For some time after this, Ruby and Bulbul were left in peace. The thieves hid themselves in the wood, tended to their bumps, bruises and stings, and kept out of their way.

Ruby began to think that they were never coming back. After all, she had tricked them into working the land, and now she had stopped them twice from getting their hands on the gold. Surely now they would have had enough?

But Ruby was mistaken …

Exactly a month later, one warm summer's evening, Ruby and Bulbul were in their beds, sound asleep. Suddenly Ruby began to stir. At first, she thought she'd been woken up by Bulbul's rumbling snores. But then she realised there were voices outside the window.

Ruby's heart sank. "It's the thieves!" she thought. "They have come back for our gold!"

Just for a moment, Ruby felt very scared. She needed a weapon to defend herself. Quickly, Ruby hopped out of bed and went over to the cupboard where Bulbul kept his barber's razor.

The only person Bulbul shaved now was himself, and he still couldn't manage it without nicking his ear or cutting his face.

Clutching the razor in her hand, Ruby stood behind the open wooden shutters, and waited.

Outside the window Karan looked sternly at his men.

"We're not going to fail this time," he said. "Raju, you creep into the house and get the gold. Mohan's messed up too many times."

"Huh, that's not fair," Mohan mumbled crossly into his beard.

"I'll get the gold, boss," Raju boasted. "Don't you worry."

He swaggered over to the window and began to climb in.

A moment later, Ruby saw a shadowy figure climbing into the bedroom. Immediately, she lashed out with the razor. She'd only meant to frighten the thief, but in the dark, she sliced a tiny piece off the tip of his nose.

"OWWWW!" the thief moaned. He

fell backwards out of the window, and landed on the ground with a thud.

"What's the matter with you, Raju?" Karan hissed crossly, hauling the man to his feet. "Where's the gold?"

"I'm bleeding!" groaned Raju, blood dripping from the end of his nose.

"You must have bumped your nose on the wooden shutter, you idiot!" sniggered Mohan, and the other thieves laughed.

Karan scowled at Mohan. "Well, if you think you're so clever, *you* can go next," he snapped.

"All right, I will," Mohan said defiantly. "And this time I *will* get the gold!"

Inside the house, Ruby waited, clutching the razor. This time she would aim for the thief's nose!

Mohan was climbing in at the window. A moment later he too fell backwards on to the ground with a shriek of pain, clutching his bleeding nose.

"Ssh!" Karan scolded furiously. "Do you want to wake the whole village?"

"You must have bumped your nose on the wooden shutter, you idiot!" said Raju sarcastically, as the other thieves tried not to laugh too loudly.

"This is ridiculous!" Karan fumed. "Gurbeet, you try next."

But every time one of the thieves climbed through the window, exactly the same thing happened. Ruby's razor flashed, and the thief fell backwards with a bleeding nose.

By the time the sixth thief had tried, Karan was becoming rather worried. He was very vain, and didn't want his looks ruined by having the tip of his nose cut off.

"You lot are the most useless bunch of thieves in the world!" he growled. "We'll give up for tonight."

Moaning, groaning and bleeding, the band of thieves made their way back to the wood.

Laughing triumphantly to herself, Ruby replaced the razor in the cupboard. Then she lit an oil lamp and, by its light, she gathered up the nosetips and hid them in a sandalwood box.

She slipped back into bed, congratulating herself on having outwitted the thieves yet again. Bulbul was still snoring. Not even the thieves' yells had woken him up.

"I'm sure that's the last we've seen of

them," Ruby thought with glee. "I've worked their fingers to the bone, they've eaten my rubbish, they've been stung all over and now I've cut off the tips of their noses! They won't come back any more now."

But Ruby was wrong. Karan was still utterly determined to get his hands on the gold. Word was spreading around the land that a simple village woman had got the better of Karan's gang, and the thieves were becoming the target of jokes.

Karan was very embarrassed. His gang had been the most feared for miles around before Ruby came along, and now they were a laughing-stock. This time he was determined to get the better of her.

So he waited a week or two until his men's noses had healed up, and then, in the dead of night, they set out once again for Ruby and Bulbul's village.

When they arrived at the house, Karan could hardly believe his luck. Because the night was warm and humid, Ruby and Bulbul had decided to sleep in the courtyard. They had dragged their beds outside, and both of them were fast asleep.

"Shall we search the house for the gold?" Mohan asked in a low voice.

Karan shook his head. "No, I've got a much better idea," he replied. "We'll kidnap the barber's wife and hold her to ransom. Pick up the bed and carry her away!"

All seven thieves surrounded the bed, picked it up and put it on their heads. Then they carried Ruby, still sleeping, out of the courtyard and along the dust track towards the city.

Chapter Five

Ruby began to stir. She'd been having a very strange dream about her bed growing legs and walking out of the courtyard. Strangely, it felt as if her bed really was moving along by itself. Puzzled, Ruby yawned and opened her eyes.

Suddenly she realised that it wasn't a dream after all. By the pale light of the moon overhead, she could see that her bed was being carried along by Karan and his band of thieves.

Ruby shut her eyes quickly before the thieves noticed she was awake. For a moment she felt terrified. Her heart thumped, and she trembled all over.

"They're kidnapping me!" she thought, "and they'll make Bulbul hand over the gold as ransom. What shall I do?"

But for once, Ruby was so scared, she couldn't think of a clever plan at all. At that moment the thieves, panting and sweating, came to a halt under a big banyan tree.

Immediately Ruby saw a way to escape. She reached up, grabbed one of the branches and swung herself into the tree. She left her quilt bunched up on the bed, so it looked as if someone was still asleep underneath it.

"My arms are dropping off!" Mohan grumbled. "This bed's as heavy as a cartful of bricks. Can't we stop and take a rest?"

"All right," Karan agreed reluctantly. "Put the bed down over there. But one of us will have to stay awake and guard the prisoner while the others sleep."

"Not me," Mohan said instantly. "I'm exhausted."

"So am I," Raju chimed in.

"Well, I'm not doing it," snorted Gurbeet.

"Quiet!" Karan hissed. "I'll guard

the prisoner." He glanced over at the bunched-up quilt. "That way, I can be sure she won't escape."

The other thieves stretched out under the banyan tree, and were asleep within minutes. Peering down from the tree at the robber captain below her, Ruby wondered how she could escape.

She stared down at Karan. He looked very vain with that long, curly, black moustache. Ruby remembered how, earlier, Karan hadn't wanted to take the chance of getting his nose tip cut off.

He obviously thought a great deal of himself – and that gave her an idea. Drawing her scarf across her face, she began to sing sweetly.

Startled, Karan glanced upwards. Immediately he spotted the veiled figure in the tree.

"No woman from the village would be out alone at this time of night," he muttered. "It must be a fairy spirit.

And from the look of it, she seems to have taken quite a fancy to me!"

Chuckling, Karan smoothed his moustache, jumped to his feet and began to strut about under the tree, as vain as any peacock. "Come down, fairy, and tell me your name," he called softly.

Ruby ignored him and continued singing. Karan grinned.

"Well, then I'll come to you, my beauty!" he said. He shinned up the tree, and sat on the branch next to Ruby, who drew her veil round her face and turned away.

"Now, won't you tell me your name?"

Ruby shook her head.

"I mustn't talk to you," she said in sweet, fairy-like tones. "Everyone knows men are not to be trusted!"

"Won't you give me a chance at least?" wheedled Karan, leaning towards her.

Ruby considered this. "Well," she began, "close your eyes and put out your tongue. Then I can touch it with the tip of mine. Fairies can taste if men are telling lies, you know!"

Thinking that this was just an excuse to kiss him, Karan grinned, closed his eyes and put out his tongue. Immediately Ruby bit it hard, and bit the tip right off.

"Aaargh!" Karan roared with pain.

He let go of the branch and crashed heavily to the ground, where he lay dazed and bruised. The other thieves woke up straightaway, and leapt to their feet.

"What's going on?" Mohan cried.

Karan's tongue was hurting so much, he couldn't reply. Clutching his bleeding mouth, he pointed up into the tree.

The other thieves peered nervously upwards. But Ruby had hidden herself behind a big banyan leaf, and could not be seen.

"Maybe it's a ghost," Raju whispered.

Ruby heard this. She began to flap her veil and hoot and howl in a blood-curdling voice.

"It is a ghost!" gasped Mohan. "Let's get out of here!"

Shrieking with fear, the thieves ran off. They were so scared, they even forgot to take the bed along with them. Laughing heartily, Ruby climbed down from the tree. The thieves had her in their clutches, and she'd outwitted them yet again!

"Surely that's the last we've seen of them now!" she said to herself, as she dragged her bed home. "But if they come back again, I'll be ready for them!"

By now Karan had had more than enough of the barber's wife. He decided that there was only one way to get the gold, and that was to claim half the money through the law. So he went to the King, and asked him to decide what was fair.

Bulbul and Ruby were summoned to the royal palace to defend themselves before the court. There, in front of the King and his advisers, Karan and his band of thieves told their tale.

"She tricked us into digging and tilling that waste land," explained Karan, shooting a look of pure hatred at Ruby. "They sowed rice seed, and took home a whole pot full of gold coins. At least half that gold should be ours."

"Hear, hear!" shouted the other

thieves with approval.

"Have you anything to say in your defence?" the King asked Ruby and Bulbul.

"Er – no, Sire," yawned Bulbul. He was tired out after the long walk, and couldn't wait to get back home to bed.

"Well, I do." Ruby stepped forward fearlessly. "These men are the thieves who live in the wood outside the city walls. They have tried by every possible means to rob us of our gold, like they have robbed so many poor travellers."

"Look!" Ruby pulled the sandalwood box from under her sari, and showed it to the King. "Here are their nose tips and the tip of their leader's tongue. I had to defend myself with my husband's razor."

Shamefaced, the thieves hung their heads as the King stared at their scarred noses. Karan opened his mouth to speak, then shut it again as the King noticed his tongue-tip was missing.

"Guards, arrest these men!" the King ordered. "They've committed many crimes, and must be punished."

Struggling and cursing, the thieves were carried off. Then the King turned to Ruby and Bulbul.

"Bulbul," he said with a smile. "I have a great favour to grant you. I would like you to become my Chief Minister. You'll live here with me at the court, and you and your wife will never be poor again."

"Sire," Bulbul stammered nervously, "that sounds like very hard work! I mean, I'm not worthy of such a great honour."

"Of course you're not," said the King with a smile, "but Ruby is!" He took Ruby's hand and turned to his court.

"Ruby has taught us a valuable lesson," the King announced. "She has shown us that an intelligent mind can outwit even the strongest opponent – in short, that brains are better than brawn. And with such a clever wife, Bulbul will never do a foolish thing or make a bad decision as long as she is alive!"

About the Author

Narinder Dhami was born in Wolverhampton to an Indian father and an English mother. Narinder studied English at Birmingham University and went on to teach in primary schools for nine years. She now writes full time but often visits schools to talk about her books.

Her most recent books include *Changing Places*, *Bindhi Babes* and the novelisation of *Bend It Like Beckham*.

Narinder Dhami now lives in Cambridge with her husband, Robert, and their five cats.

Another White Wolves title you might enjoy ...

Taliesin

retold by Maggie Pearson

A man drinks from the magic cauldron of knowledge and is reborn as Taliesin: magician, prophet and trickster.

Follow Taliesin's progress as he changes the fortunes of all he encounters – for better and for worse.

Another White Wolves title you might enjoy ...

The Path of Finn McCool
retold by Sally Prue

The giant, Finn McCool, discovers that the biggest head doesn't always hold the biggest brain in this larger-than-life comedy.

When he annoys the Little People, they warn him of an even bigger giant across the sea in Scotland. Finn makes the big mistake of setting out to find him ...

Year 5

The Path of Finn McCool • Sally Prue

The Barber's Clever Wife • Narinder Dhami

Taliesin • Maggie Pearson

Fool's Gold • David Calcutt

Time Switch • Steve Barlow and Steve Skidmore

Let's Go to London! • Kaye Umansky

Year 6

Shock Forest and Other Stories • Margaret Mahy

Sky Ship and Other Stories • Geraldine McCaughrean

Snow Horse and Other Stories • Joan Aiken

Macbeth • Tony Bradman

Romeo and Juliet • Michael Cox

The Tempest • Franzeska G. Ewart